THIS ANNUAL BELONGS TO ...

Stick your own
photo here.

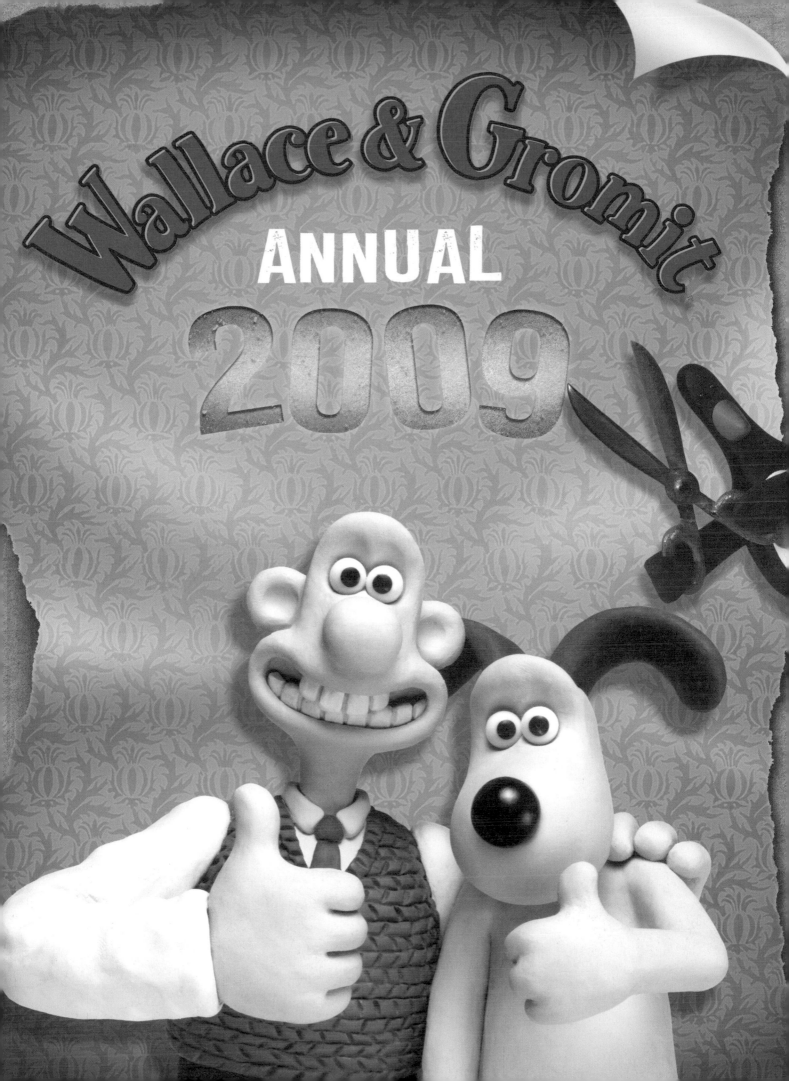

Contents

EGMONT

We bring stories to life

First published in Great Britain in 2008 by Egmont UK Limited
239 Kensington High Street, London W8 6SA

© and ™ Aardman Animations Ltd 2008. All rights reserved.
Based on characters created by Nick Park.

Written by Brenda Apsley, based on original scripts. Designed by Craig Cameron.

ISBN 978 1 4052 3916 5

1 3 5 7 9 10 8 6 4 2

Printed in Italy

Meet Wallace ...

Wallace is an inventor who's full of ideas. They sound great on paper, but what he plans to make and what he actually makes aren't always the same thing! His gadgets and machines almost always go wrong, and often get him into deep trouble.

Wallace lives at 62 West Wallaby Street, in a small town in the north. The house may look ordinary from the outside, but inside it's packed to the rafters with his labour-saving devices and gizmos, all made in the cellar workshop.

Wallace likes:

- cheese
- crackers
- his dog, Gromit
- more cheese
- more crackers

Wallace dislikes:

- not having any cheese
- not having any crackers

and Gromit

Gromit is Wallace's pet dog. But he's really much, much more than just a common canine. He doesn't speak, of course, but then he doesn't have to: one of his looks makes it obvious what he's thinking.

Gromit is brave, and loyal to a fault. Though he may not approve of his owner's hare-brained schemes, he'll always go along with them – usually because he needs to be there to get Wallace out of trouble.

Gromit likes:

- Wallace
- 'Electronics for Dogs' magazine
- curling up with a good book
- knitting

Gromit dislikes:

- Feathers McGraw

A Grand Day Out ™

One day, Wallace and Gromit were reading their favourite magazines: **CHEESE MONTHLY** and **CHEESE HOLIDAYS** for Wallace and *ELECTRONICS FOR DOGS* for Gromit.

Reading about cheese made Wallace hungry, but when he opened the fridge, his face fell. The cheese dish was empty.

"No cheese, Gromit!" he said. "This won't do. Let's go for a day out, somewhere where there's lots and lots of cheese!"

Wallace thought for a minute or two, then smiled.

"I know!" he said. "They say the Moon's made of cheese, don't they? Come on, Gromit, lad, let's get a move on. We've got a space rocket to build."

Wallace and Gromit went down to the workshop in the cellar, and set to work right away.

"Here, Gromit," Wallace said, as he cut up an old door. "Make yourself useful and prop this up for me."

When the rocket was ready, Wallace and Gromit climbed aboard. "Adjust angle of thrust," Wallace told Gromit. "Commence countdown ...
Ten ...
nine ...
eight ...
seven ...
six ...
five ...
four ...
three ...
two ...
one ...
BLAST OFF!"
Wallace looked around. "Now where did I put those crackers?"

To the Moon ...

Finding your way to the Moon is not easy, as Gromit knows, because he's the pilot of the spaceship. Wallace just gives the orders!

Can you show Gromit the quickest way through the maze to get to the Moon? Make sure you steer clear of the meteors!

EARTH
START

MOON
FINISH

When the spaceship landed on the Moon, Wallace set out a picnic and broke off a piece of Moon cheese.

"Mmm," he said. "It's like ... er ... it's like no cheese I've ever tasted."

After his Moon-cheese-sampling session, Wallace took a walk among the craters.

He didn't meet any spacemen or aliens, but he did come across a strange machine, a sort of robo-cooker.

"Hmmm," said Wallace, looking at the 10p coin slot on the front of the machine. "Very interesting. I wonder what this thing does? I think I'll give it a try."

Wallace put a 10p coin in the slot on the robo-cooker.

He waited and waited, but nothing happened. "Daylight robbery," said Wallace. "They always nick your money, these flipping slot machines."

But when he walked away, the robo-cooker made a strange humming sound, and turned around.

It saw Wallace eating more Moon cheese, promptly produced a baseball bat, and was just about to bop him with it when the money ran out, and it stopped moving.

"Hmmm," said Wallace, when he saw the machine standing beside him.

He took the baseball bat, put another 10p in the slot, and waited.

As before, nothing happened, so Wallace picked up his picnic basket and started to fill it with Moon cheese to take home.

As he and Gromit walked back to the rocket, the machine suddenly came to life and scuttled after them.

"Quick!" said Wallace. "Hurry, Gromit. That robo-cooker-thingy's after us, and it doesn't look too friendly!"

"Crikey! Look, Gromit, it's trying to get aboard!" said Wallace, as he saw the robo-cooker scuttling towards the spaceship. "Lock the door and commence emergency countdown, Gromit! Ten, nine, eight, seven, six, five, four, three, two, one ... BLAST OFF!"

The rocket took off into space, and the Moon – and the robo-cooker – were soon left far, far behind.

Wallace settled down for a cheesy snack.

"Set the co-ordinates for 62 West Wallaby Street, Gromit," he said. "I think that's quite enough space travel for one day ..."

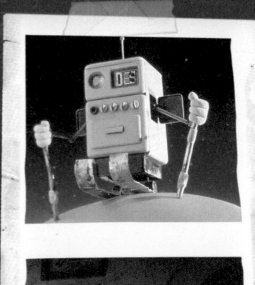

"Home, Gromit!"

Can you show Gromit the way back to Earth from the Moon? This time, make sure you don't steer the spaceship into any black holes!

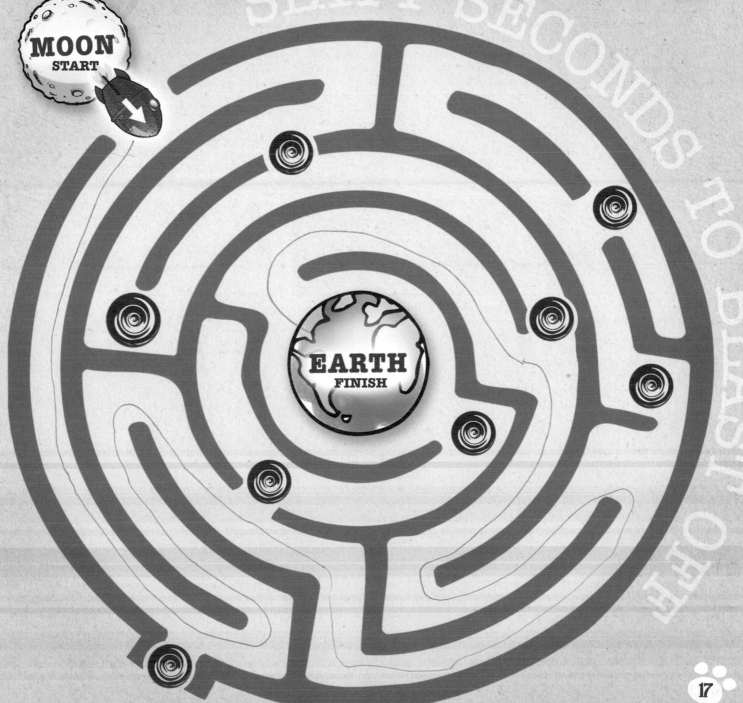

MOON
START

EARTH
FINISH

SIXTY SECONDS TO BLAST OFF

62 WEST WALLABY STREET:

64 WEST WALLABY STREET:

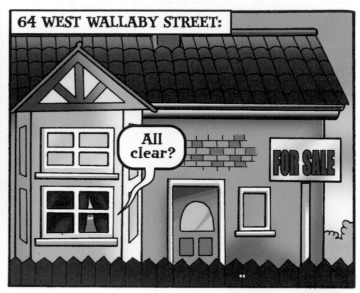

All clear?

HOUSE NEXT DOOR

FOR SALE

Looks like it, *Ena.* No sign of life, anyhow.

Good. They'll be here soon. If we're lucky, we can get 'em in and out without anyone being any the wiser. And then ...

... *Le Costa Packet,* here we come!

Just think, *Arthur* ... no more *mini-earthquakes* in the middle of the night!

No more *sub-orbital* sausages come barbecue season!

No more *projectile* paint when he's decorating!

Just sun, sea ...

"... and *normal* next-door neighbours!"

Script Simon Furman ☐ Pencils Paul Peart ☐ Inks Bambos Georgiou ☐ Colours Martin Baines ☐ Letters Jimmy Betancourt/Comicraft

THE NEXT DAY ...

As you can see, all mod cons. Plumbing's in tip top condition. Checked it all meself.

Yes, so I can see. It's ...

... er, making a *funny* noise?

TKTA

TKTA

KUUUSH!

Eek!

SPOW

FLUUSH!

THRRP

Reg, what is it? What's happenin' to me beautiful bathroom?!

It's him! Who else?

Wallace!

Waaallace!

Where's the Cheese?

Can you find these names hidden in the grid on the opposite page? They are spelled out from left to right, across the page, and from top to bottom, down the page.

FEATHERS ☐   **GROMIT** ☐   **PRESTON** ☐

SHAUN ☐   **WALLACE** ☑   **WENDOLENE** ☐

Draw a line through each name when you find it, and tick the list above. But before you get cracking, find the **CHEESE**s Wallace has misplaced. Colour in a piece of **CHEESE** for each time you find the word **CHEESE** in the grid.

There are

....

pieces of

CHEESE.

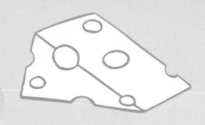

A	X	C	H	E	E	S	E	B	O
J	M	A	W	S	C	R	G	V	P
C	F	E	A	T	H	E	R	S	R
H	N	E	L	G	E	W	O	H	E
E	T	B	L	O	E	K	M	A	S
E	U	E	A	Y	S	X	I	U	T
S	O	M	C	D	E	Q	T	N	O
E	C	H	E	E	S	E	H	I	N
L	W	E	N	D	O	L	E	N	E
F	O	Z	P	C	H	E	E	S	E

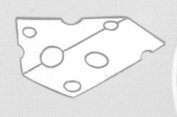

ANSWERS: There are 5 CHEESES in the grid.

THE CURSE OF THE WERE-RABBIT

Lady Campanula Tottington's annual Giant Vegetable Competition was under threat, not from greenfly or mildew, but from rabbits that were guzzling all the vegetables.

Would Wallace and Gromit's Anti-Pesto Humane Pest Control team be able to banish the hungry bunnies?

"Of course we will!" said Wallace.

Soon, our heroes had hundreds of bunnies in Wallace's super-charged Bun-Vac 6000, which sucked up 125 rpm (rabbits per minute).

"My hero!" said Lady Tottington.

Wallace used his Mind Manipulation-O-Matic to brainwash the bunnies into hating vegetables. "Veg bad, veg bad," he said. "Say no to carrots!"

But that night, the vegetables were guzzled again. This time the culprits weren't the bunnies, but a ginormous were-rabbit!

"Oh, heck, we've created a monster!" said Wallace. "When the Moon comes out, that big rabbit called Hutch turns into a were-rabbit!"

Later, Gromit followed huge paw-prints into Wallace's bedroom, which was full of vegetables and bunny droppings. That meant just one thing: WALLACE was the were-rabbit! His brain waves had got mixed up with Hutch's when he'd tested the Mind Manipulation-O-Matic!

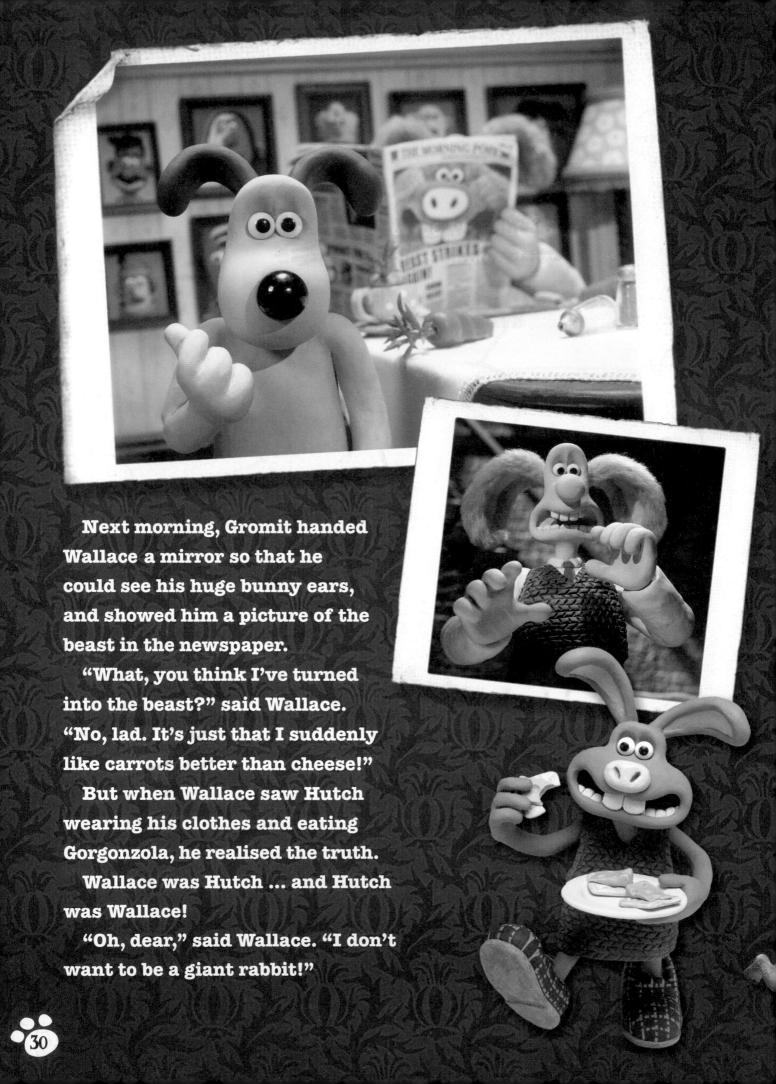

Next morning, Gromit handed Wallace a mirror so that he could see his huge bunny ears, and showed him a picture of the beast in the newspaper.

"What, you think I've turned into the beast?" said Wallace. "No, lad. It's just that I suddenly like carrots better than cheese!"

But when Wallace saw Hutch wearing his clothes and eating Gorgonzola, he realised the truth.

Wallace was Hutch ... and Hutch was Wallace!

"Oh, dear," said Wallace. "I don't want to be a giant rabbit!"

BUNNY DROPPINGS

Can you guess who's hiding? Colour in ONLY the shapes with a bunny dropping in them to find out if you're right.

31

That night, when the Moon came out, Wallace's hands became furry paws, then oversized feet burst out of his slippers, and he sprouted a fluffy bunny tail.

Seconds later, his transformation into the giant were-rabbit was complete!

When Victor Quartermaine arrived to shoot the beast, Gromit shoved the mega-bunny outside, and it hopped off as Victor fired: BLAM!

"Got 'im!" Victor announced. "Now Lady Tottington's Giant Vegetable Competition can go ahead as planned, and I'll be in her good books!"

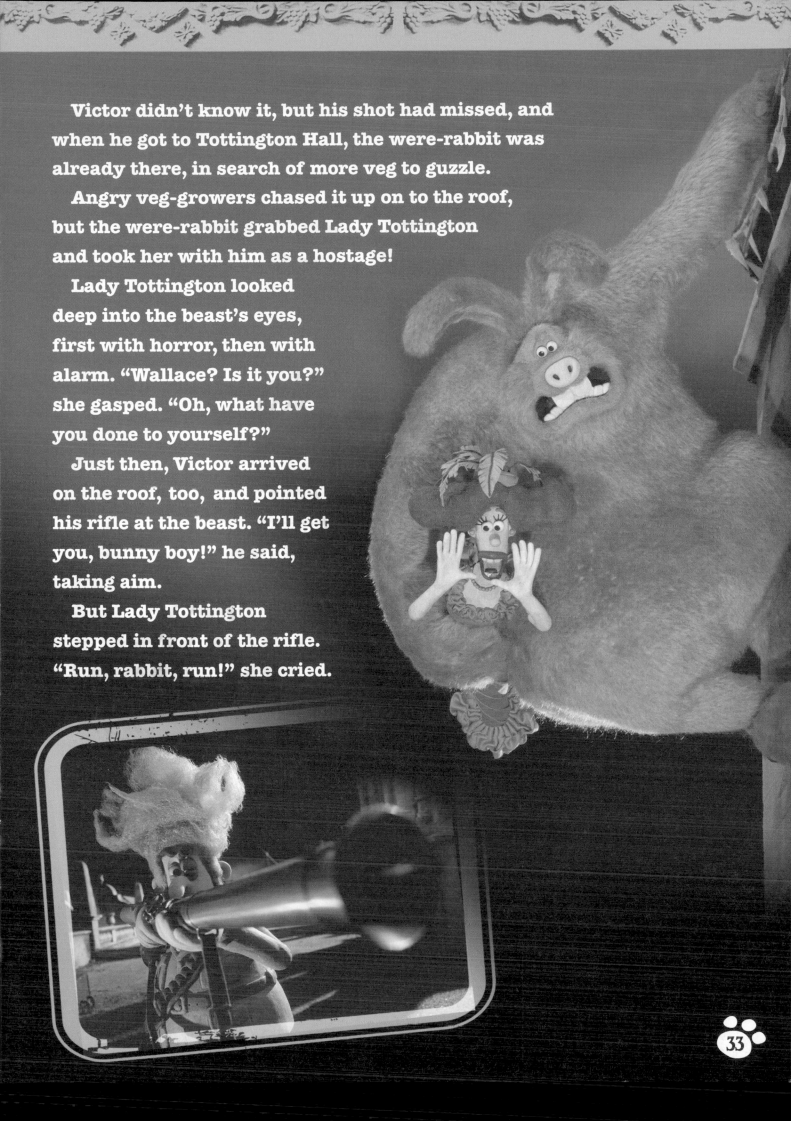

Victor didn't know it, but his shot had missed, and when he got to Tottington Hall, the were-rabbit was already there, in search of more veg to guzzle.

Angry veg-growers chased it up on to the roof, but the were-rabbit grabbed Lady Tottington and took her with him as a hostage!

Lady Tottington looked deep into the beast's eyes, first with horror, then with alarm. "Wallace? Is it you?" she gasped. "Oh, what have you done to yourself?"

Just then, Victor arrived on the roof, too, and pointed his rifle at the beast. "I'll get you, bunny boy!" he said, taking aim.

But Lady Tottington stepped in front of the rifle. "Run, rabbit, run!" she cried.

The were-rabbit jumped to the edge of the roof and looked down.

"Stand back!" PC Mackintosh told the crowd watching from below. "There may be a large bunny dropping!"

And there was, as the beast jumped, and landed in the cheese tent.

Victor ended up there, too, helped by a wallop on the bonce from Lady Tottington.

Hearing the angry mob outside, Gromit decided that he had to do something to save were-Wallace.

He dressed a still-dazed Victor in a huge bunny costume, and pushed him outside.

"There's the beast!" cried the angry veg growers. "After it!"

Slowly, bit by bit, the were-rabbit transformed back into Wallace, but he lay still and lifeless – until Gromit held a piece of extra-super-stinky cheese under his nose.

That did the trick! "Cheese!" said Wallace. "I'm me again! Well done, old pal!"

And so, Lady Tottington decided to turn Tottington Hall into a Bunny Sanctuary.

"Fire up the old Bun-Vac 6000, Gromit!" said Wallace, and the captured bunnies were blown back out to freedom.

The last to emerge was Hutch!

"Cheeeeeeeeese!" he cried.

A CLOSE SNIP

Wallace! What have you got there, my friend?

Well, Toni – I was thinking about how you were short staffed – and I came up with a 'fringe benefit'!

When you're cutting hair, you don't have time to make the tea, that sort of thing – So instead of having these ladies sit under the dryers, all ignored ...

... Why not use the KWIK-COIFFURE!

What is it! *A hair dryer?*

It's a 'cut above' a hair dryer! Here you go, my dear – put this on your head.

And presto, with one click of the switch ...

--everything you need in one machine!

MORE - TEA - DEAR?

WOULD - YOU - LIKE - THIS - WEEK'S - MAGAZINE?

This is MARVELLOUS! I can do twice as much now in half the time!

ERROR - ERROR - ERROR

HSSSSSSSTT

Oh dear - that doesn't sound good!

Gromit, pull the plug ...

... Laaadddd!!!!

CHANGE - STYLE - MORE - FUNKY

36 · Story Tony Lee · Pencils Brian Williamson · Inks Bambos Georgiou · Colours Martin Baines · Letters Jimmy Betancourt/Comicraft

A CLOSE SHAVE ™

There was trouble in town. Someone was stealing all the sheep, and soon knitting wool was in very short supply, which was bad news for a keen knitter like Gromit.

One day, the owner of the wool shop, Wendolene Ramsbottom, called Wallace and Gromit's Wash 'n' Go Window Cleaning Service and asked them to come and clean the shop windows.

"Be right with you!" said Wallace. "Come on, Gromit!" Wallace liked Wendolene on sight. But he did wonder why she had more balls of wool than she could handle ...

All the Wool in the World

"Do let me help you," said Wallace, as Wendolene
struggled to count the balls of wool in her shop.

Will you help, too? Colour in a ball of wool for each one
in the picture, then write the number in the box.

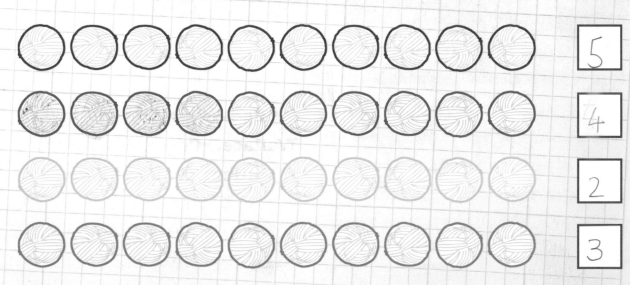

⭕⭕⭕⭕⭕⭕⭕⭕⭕⭕	5
⭕⭕⭕⭕⭕⭕⭕⭕⭕⭕	4
⭕⭕⭕⭕⭕⭕⭕⭕⭕⭕	2
⭕⭕⭕⭕⭕⭕⭕⭕⭕⭕	3

ANSWERS: There are 6 red, 7 blue, 2 yellow and 2 green balls of wool.

That afternoon, one of the stolen sheep fell out of the getaway lorry and went through the dog flap into ... 62 West Wallaby Street.

Being stolen had made the woolly fellow hungry, and he ate just about everything in the house: newspapers, plants, Wallace's cheese ... and Gromit's bone.

"He's been at me cheese!" said Wallace in horror, when he and Gromit got home.

But Wallace liked the sheep, and put him in his Knit-O-Matic machine for a wash.

Gromit turned the machine on, but it went into 'shave' mode and fleeced the shivering sheep, presenting Wallace with a jumper made of the wool!

"Give him the jumper, Gromit," said Wallace. "We'll call him Shaun."

Next day, Gromit found out that Preston, Wendolene's dog, was the sheep-stealer!

His plan was to use the wool for Wendolene's shop and turn the sheep into dog food!

Gromit managed to rescue all the sheep. But sneaky Preston made it look as if it was Gromit who had stolen them, and he was arrested and put on trial!

KILLER DOG GROMIT CAUGHT

Wallace read in the newspaper, then:

SHEEP DOG TRIAL CONTINUES

and finally:

GROMIT GETS LIFE

"Oh, Gromit!" said Wallace.

Gromit was in his prison cell when he got a parcel from Wallace: a 5,000-piece jigsaw puzzle!

It took him days to do, but when he fitted the pieces together he found a secret message:

FRIDAY NIGHT, 8PM.
BE READY.
A FRIEND.

Gromit checked: it was Friday, eight o'clock and, sure enough, seconds later, his friend Shaun the sheep cut through the bars of the cell window.

Gromit made his Great Escape!

Just then, he and Wallace spotted Preston in his lorry with another batch of stolen sheep in the back, and they set off after him on the motorbike and sidecar.

Wallace drove close enough to free the sheep, and they all ended up riding on the motorbike ...

A Tight Squeeze

It was a very tight squeeze on Wallace's getaway motorbike!

How many sheep hitched a ride with Wallace?

Count them, and circle the number.

1 2 3 4 5 6 7 8 9 10 11 12 13 14 15 16 17 18 (19) 20

ANSWER: There are 19 sheep.

When Preston saw the sheep-laden motorbike following him, he released the back door flap of the lorry. Then he braked so suddenly that Wallace drove the motorbike and sidecar, and all the sheep, into the back of the lorry. Result!

Preston drove to his factory, where he put Wallace and the others on the conveyor belt that led to his dog-food machine!

But clever Shaun pressed a switch, and it was Preston who was tipped into the 'close shave' section of the machine, emerging as a snarling cyber dog!

Shaun pushed him into the gnashing jaws of the Mutton-o-matic. When he came out, it was in the form of springs, nuts and bolts, in a neatly canned body.

Gromit was pardoned, and Wallace rebuilt Preston, this time as a harmless dog-on-wheels.

A few days later, Wendolene took him to visit Wallace and Gromit.

"Thank you, Wallace," she said. "Now Preston is just like he used to be."

Wallace had hoped that he and Wendolene might become more than just good friends – until she told him that she didn't like cheese!

"Oh, well, Gromit," said Wallace later. "More cheese for me and you, lad!"

DRAW Wallace

Draw your own picture of Wallace. It's easy if you do it step-by-step.

1 Start with a finger shape, and add a circle for a nose.

2 Add two circles for eyes,

3 a banana mouth, and a curved shoulder line.

4 Add ears, cheeks, neck and shirt collar,

5 then eyeballs, eyebrows, inner ears, mouth and clothes.

6 Finally, draw rows of teeth, pattern the jumper and you have – Wallace!

You can colour in
your drawing if you like,
using these colours.

Wallace by

Gregor..

... and into the afternoon, with sunny periods throughout our region ...

Piffle!

... and tonight, warm and dry, with the outlook summery.

Back to you, Fiona.

Poppycock!

LUNCH BREAK AT 62 WEST WALLABY STREET ...

That chap wouldn't know a *warm front* from a *hole in the ground!*

Do the daily check, Gromit, if you don't mind.

"I DON'T CARE WHAT THE WEATHER MAN SAYS..."

Sunny periods, he says! *Sunny periods?*

Writer Dan Abnett  Pencils Brian Williamson Inks Bambos Georgiou Colours John Burns Letters Jimmy Betancourt/Comicraft

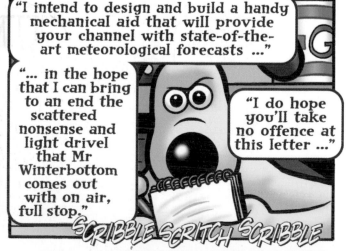

THE LOCAL TV STATION, A FEW DAYS LATER ...

"... I am only trying to help out. Yours, Wallace, brackets local inventor, close brackets."

Heh heh! That's *quite* a hoot, don't you think, Ron?

Do I *hailstones*, Mr Fortesque!

Come *on*, Ron. It's just a piece of fun. I'm thinking of running a little "on the lighter side" item about it at the end of the news.

But that'll make Ron Winterbottom look like a *nincompoop!*

I think the boat's already *sailed* on that one, Ron.

May I see that?

62, West Wallaby Street

RAP TAPA TAP TAP

62

Hello? Anyone home? Mr Wallace? I was wanting a word with you.

RAP-TAP TAP 62

Mr Wallace? It's Ron Winterbottom, from the TV. Are you home?

Oh brr-brr-*brrilliant!*
It's no b-b-b-b-better in here!

That b-b-blessed thundercloud's *still* chasing us!

Quick! Let's t-t-take shelter in the *pantry!*

Inside, Gromit! B-b-before–

Crikey! That's a heck of a *draft* coming through there!

Help me! Are you still there? Help!

That poor blighter's *still* calling to us! We've no choice, lad. We'll just have to make a *dash* for the shed!

Any ideas?

Then no matter *what* button I pressed, it just *wouldn't* switch off!

Quickly! Shut it down before they ... they ...

"They"?

By crikey! We're going to need a bigger brolly ...

Gromit, lad, turn the machine off. Before they smell fear.

KLUNK

POP POP POP POP POP POP POP POP POP

Oh. Plug, was it?

What the dickens *is* this contraption?

If you must know, it turned out to be *harder* than I thought to build a machine to predict the weather.

It was a lot *easier* to build one that *created* weather to order instead. That way, we'd not *need* any forecasts.

Questions, Questions

How much do you know about Wallace and Gromit? Try answering these questions. All the answers are in the annual – if you know where to find them!

1 Wallace and Gromit live in West Wallaby Street. Is their house number:

a 64 ☐

b 62, or ☐

c 63? ☑

2 In I Don't Care What the Weatherman Says, who is the weatherman?

a Ron Winterbottom ☐

b Rick Sidebottom, or ☐

c Tommy Shufflebottom? ☐

3 What is the name of Gromit's favourite magazine?

a Bone Hunting ☐

b Cheese Monthly, or ☐

c Electronics for Dogs? ☑

4 What kind of animal is Feathers McGraw?

a a penguin ☑

b a polar bear, or ☐

c a pilchard? ☐

5 What is the name of the owner of the wool shop?

a Wendy Ollerenshaw ☑

b Wendolene Ramsbottom, or ☐

c Gwendolyn Gasbottom? ☐

6 What kind of animal is Preston?

a a sheep dog ☐

b a cyber dog, or ☑

c a police dog? ☐

7 Is the owner of the Bunny Sanctuary:

a Lady Tottington ☑

b Lady Bottington, or ☐

c Lady Quartermaine? ☐

THE WRONG TROUSERS

It was Gromit's birthday.

"I've got a special surprise present to give you after breakfast," said Wallace. "Drink your tea."

The surprise made Gromit's ears stand on end!

"Techno Trousers, to take you walkies!" said Wallace. "I attach your lead here, like this, then set the dial to Walkies: 20 minutes, and off you go!"

The Techno Trousers set off, pulling Gromit behind them.

"Fast, eh?" said Wallace. "Have a nice walk, Gromit!"

When Gromit got back from his techno-walkies, Wallace had another surprise for him: a penguin lodger called Feathers McGraw!

Feathers moved into Gromit's room, and Gromit moved out into the kennel!

"He seems pleasant enough," said Wallace, as Feathers brought his slippers. "Cheer up, Gromit!"

Gromit didn't make a sound, but his face said it all.

Next morning, the penguin put a still-sleepy Wallace into the Techno Trousers, and he was walked out of the house!

"What have you done, Gromit?" cried Wallace. "These aren't my trousers! They're the the **WRONG trousers!** Stop them, lad!"

But Gromit didn't hear. He had seen that he wasn't wanted any more, and had left home.

At that very moment he was looking in horror at a poster with Feathers' picture on it.

WANTED it said, **FOR ROBBERY!**

That night, when Wallace was fast asleep, Feathers put him into the Techno Trousers again, and sent him to steal the famous Blue Diamond!

Everything went according to plan – until the burglar alarm went off – NAH-NAH! NAH-NAH! and woke Wallace.

"What's going on?" he asked, as Feathers walked him – and the Blue Diamond – back to West Wallaby Street.

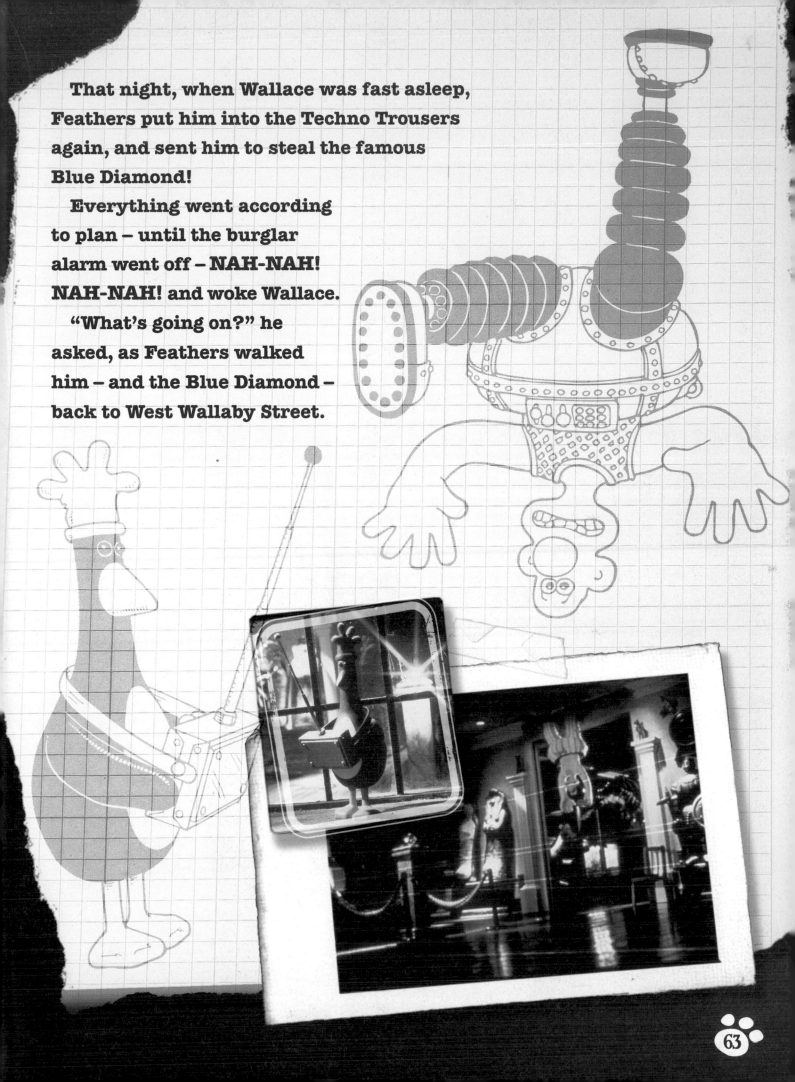

Brave-as-a-lion Gromit went home and managed to rescue Wallace, but Feathers pulled a gun on him, and made his escape on Wallace's train set.

Wallace and Gromit gave chase, and after a hair-, fur- and feather-raising ride, the train crashed, and Feathers flew off into the air, landing in ... a milk bottle.

"We bottled Feathers once and for all, Gromit, lad!" said Wallace. "Thank you, old friend."

When all the excitement of being a hero was over, Gromit settled down to read the paper.

FEATHERS McGRAW BACK INSIDE said the headline.

"The reward money means we don't have to take in any more lodgers, so you can have your old room back," said Wallace. "Lodgers are more trouble than they're worth, if you ask me. Now, I fancy some cheese, Gromit. What d'you say to a bit of Gorgonzola?"

Techno Trousers

Wallace's Techno Trousers are on the loose and totally out of control!
Follow the instructions to guide them through the grid on the opposite page.

∧ 1 = go up 1 square

∨ 2 = go down 2 squares

> 3 = go right 3 squares

< 4 = go left 4 squares

Who are the Techno Trousers heading for?

Follow these clues line by line to find out!

∧4	<3	∧2	>3	∨1
>1	∧3	<4	∧1	>6
∨2	<1	∨6	>4	∧1
<2	∧5	>2	∧2	<2
∧1	<5	∧1	>7	∧1
<3	∧1	<5	∨3	<1

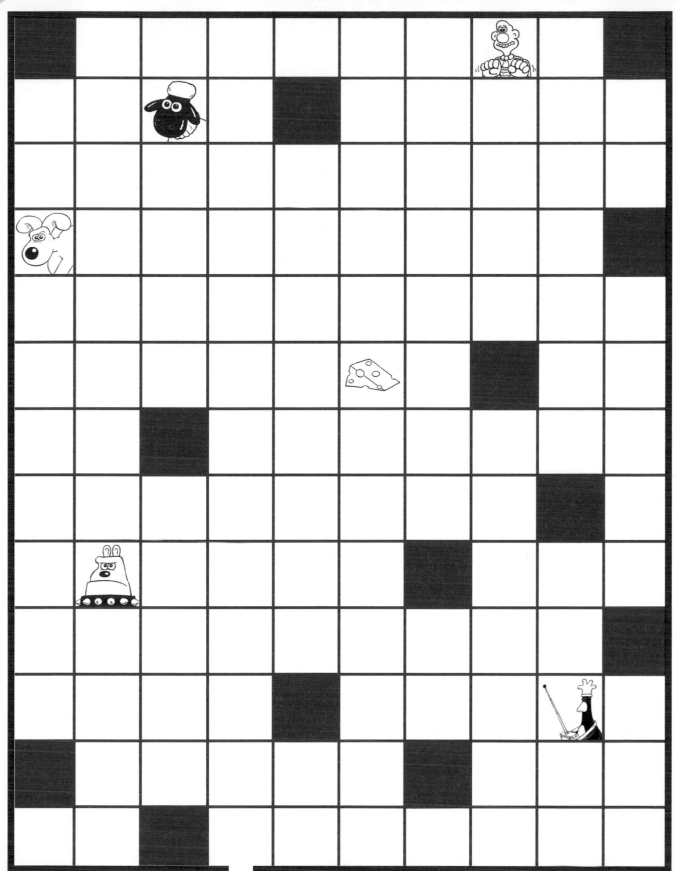

START HERE

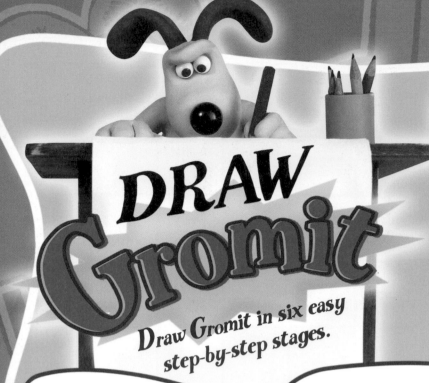

DRAW Gromit

Draw Gromit in six easy step-by-step stages.

1 Start with an egg shape,

2 then add two overlapping circles,

3 three circles for eyes and nose, and a face outline.

4 Add a neck and four legs,

5 then two floppy ears, eyeballs, eyebrows, toes and a tail.

6 Finally, copy the shading lines, fill in the nose and you have – Gromit!

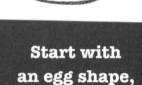

**Colour in your drawing if you like.
These are the colours you need:**

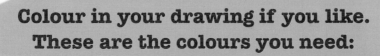

Gromit by

Gregor
....

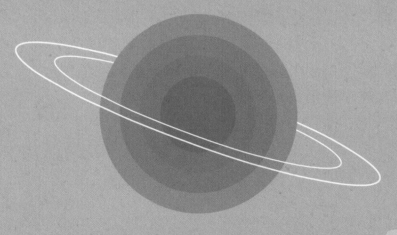

SET CO-ORDINATES
FOR 62 WEST
WALLABY STREET